John Mouse

raises the alarm

D1027282

Copyright 1973 Roger Hargreaves

Published by Fabbri & Partners Ltd., 24 Old Bond Street, London W1X 3DA

It was the middle of the night, and everybody was asleep in Appletree Cottage.

Mr Simpkin was fast asleep in his bedroom.

He was dreaming about being able to fly like a bird through the sky.

In his dream he was flapping his arms and soaring high above the open countryside.

It was a beautiful dream!

Ginger the cat was fast asleep in the kitchen.

He was dreaming about chasing a dog, and the dog being frightened and hiding up a tree.

What a lovely dream for a cat to dream!

And somebody else was fast asleep that night in Appletree Cottage.

The Mouse family!

Mr and Mrs Mouse were asleep.

Grandpa Mouse was asleep.

The Mouse twins, Sophie and Amelia, were asleep in their cots.

And John Mouse was asleep too.

He was dreaming about riding an elephant.

What a funny dream for a mouse to dream!

Suddenly in the quiet of the night, there was a small noise.

A sort of breaking glass noise.

This woke John Mouse from his elephant dream and he got up, rubbed his eyes with his paws, yawned, and went to see what was happening.

He opened his tiny front door, which leads out into Mr Simpkin's dining room, and peeped out.

And what do you think he saw?

A burglar!

A big fat horrid burglar who had broken the dining room window of Appletree Cottage and was climbing into the room.

John Mouse's heart went bump bump bump and he felt very small and very frightened.

"Oh dear" he squeaked silently to himself "What am I to do?"

The burglar tiptoed quietly and cautiously across the dining room looking for something to steal.

John Mouse, hiding in the shadows, watched him.

"I must do something" he thought "I must go and wake up Mr Simpkin!"

So he ran as quietly as he could, even quieter than a mouse normally runs, out of the dining room and up the stairs.

Now, as you know, stairs in a house aren't built mouse-sized, they're people-sized. And John Mouse, being mouse-sized of course, had a terrible job getting upstairs.

But eventually, puffing and panting, he did.

He ran into Mr Simpkin's bedroom.

John Mouse stood by the side of the bed and squeaked. "Squeak" he squeaked "Squeak squeak squeak".

Mr Simpkin stayed fast asleep, still dreaming.

"Oh dear me" thought John Mouse "SQUEAKSQUEAKSQUEAK SQUEAKSQUEAKSQUEAKSQUEAK SQUEAKSQUEAKSQUEAK!"

Mr Simpkin slept on.

"Oh dear me" thought John Mouse again "I must go and wake up Ginger the cat!"

So he ran as fast as his paws would carry him out of the bedroom and down the stairs and in through the dining room door.

Just as the burglar was coming out of the dining room door.

John Mouse looked up, and saw to his horror the burglar's big boot about to come down on top of him and squash him.

Luckily John Mouse is a very quick thinking mouse, and he managed to jump out of the way.

The burglar, carrying some silver knives and forks he had stolen from the dining room, didn't notice the small figure of John Mouse, and went off across the hall into Mr Simpkin's study.

John Mouse stood by the dining room door with his heart going bump bump bump again.

Then he ran to the kitchen to wake Ginger the cat.

Ginger the cat was still dreaming.

John Mouse stood by his basket and squeaked at the top of his squeak. "SQUEAKSQUEAKSQUEAKSQUEAK SQUEAK!"

Ginger the cat slept on.

John Mouse even tugged Ginger's whiskers, but still Ginger slept on.

Then John Mouse saw a ball of string, and that gave John Mouse an idea.

We said John Mouse was a very quick thinking mouse didn't we?

John Mouse rolled the ball of string across the kitchen floor and tied it to the leg of the kitchen cupboard.

Then he rolled the ball of string, unwinding it as he went, across the kitchen and into the dining room.

Then he wound the string around the leg of a chair.

Then he took the string across to another chair and tied the other end of the piece of string to that chair leg.

Then he hid.

Then he waited.

The big fat burglar by this time had stolen a lovely old clock from the study, and a box full of money from Mr Simpkin's desk, as well as the knives and forks from the dining room.

The burglar grinned a foxy grin.

Now it was time to go, and picking up his bag of swag (you know what swag is don't you?) he went out of the study, and across the hall, and into the dining room and towards the window.

Suddenly

Crash! The burglar tripped over the string.

Bang! The burglar fell to the floor.

Wallop! The burglar hit his head.

"Ouch!" The burglar said.

Tug! The string pulled the kitchen cupboard.

And up into the air went all the cups and saucers and saucepans and knives and forks and spoons and rolling pins and everything from the kitchen cupboard.

Ding. Dong. Clatter. Crash. Clash. Chink. Clink.

They all fell on to Ginger the cat.

"Meow" screeched Ginger with more of an "Ow" than a "Me".

"What?" Mr Simpkin woke up.

Jump! Mr Simpkin jumped out of bed.

Hurry! Mr Simpkin ran downstairs.

"Ooo!" The burglar sat on the floor rubbing his head.

"Got you!" Mr Simpkin seized the burglar.

"Squeak! Squeak! Squeak! Squeak! Squeak!" exclaimed Mr and Mrs Mouse and Grandpa Mouse and Sophie Mouse and Amelia Mouse who had all got up to see what the hullabaloo was all about.

"Good" squeaked John Mouse.

Then Mr Simpkin called the police, who arrested the burglar and took him away.

Later, after John Mouse had told his family all about everything, and after Mr Simpkin had tidied up and wondered who it was that tied the string that raised the alarm, everybody went back to bed.

All was peace and quiet in Appletree Cottage. Mr Simpkin was dreaming about flying.

Ginger was dreaming about chasing dogs.

And John Mouse, with a little mousey smile on his face, dreamed a dream that went Crash Bang Wallop Ouch Tug Ding Dong Clatter Crash Clash Chink Clink Meow (with more of an "Ow" than a "Me") What Jump Hurry Ooo Got you Squeak Squeak Squeak Squeak Squeak Good!

And that's the end of this John Mouse story!